STORIES BY KATHRYN JACKSON
PICTURES BY RICHARD SCARRY

The Animals' Merry Christmas

GOLDEN PRESS · NEW YORK
WESTERN PUBLISHING COMPANY, INC., RACINE, WISCONSIN

CONTENTS

A LITTLE deer came skipping home through the snowy woods. His eyes were still shining from the wonderful things he had seen. His heart felt as light as a snowflake, and as warm as he always felt close to his mother's side.

"Oh, Mother!" he cried. "I went to the town and peeped in the window of a house. There was a tree inside, glittering and shining, with stars caught in its branches—red and green ones, blue and white. And it was all hung with bright balls that sparkled the light all over the room!"

The mother deer nodded her head slowly. Her eyes shone, too.

"That was a Christmas tree," she said softly. "At Christmas time, people deck their trees with lights and toys and shining things—"

"Christmas tree!" whispered the little deer. "Oh, Mother, I want a Christmas tree!"

The mother deer pawed the snowy ground thoughtfully. Oh, how much she wanted a tree for her baby! At last an idea came to her.

"Follow me," she said. She took her baby farther into the woods, and showed him a small green tree in a little clearing.

Christmas Tree

"We'll put berries on the branches. We'll put tasty shoots on them and tender roots."

The little deer helped. He worked busily. But when the tree was dressed, it was not bright and shining like the tree in town.

"Never mind," said his mother. "Wait until morning. Then we'll come to look at it again."

Soon the baby deer was back at home, tucked closely to his mother's side. Soon he was asleep in the dark, snow-clad woods. And just as the sun came up, his mother awakened him.

Deep into the woods they went on their quiet feet. Close to the clearing they stopped and peeped in. The little deer opened his eyes and his mouth. Icicles hung from his Christmas tree, shining with sunrise. Snowflakes sparkled on it, in red and blue and green. And on all the branches were dozens of bright singing birds, eating the berries and roots and shoots.

"Merry Christmas!" they sang on that early Christmas morning. "Merry Christmas!" they chattered between bites.

The little deer nuzzled his nose in his mother's neck.

"It's a beautiful tree!" he whispered. "Much more beautiful than the tree in town!"

And still the birds sang, and the mother deer smiled happily, and one by one, the other animals came through the woods to look at the little deer's wonderful singing Christmas tree.

A Pig's Christmas

A pig went to market,
His heart full of glee,
To buy his friends presents.
"Not ONE thing for me!"
Said he, said he, said the pig.

He saw some red mittens
With green Christmas trees.
"What size?" asked the clerk.
"MY size, if you please!"
Said he, said he, said the pig.

"I'll buy me this sweater,
These boxing gloves, too,
This sled which just suits me!
Some taffy to chew——"
Said he, said he, said the pig.

"A book and some apples
Come next on my list,
And I think I should have
A real watch for my wrist,"
Said he, said he, said the pig.

"They're fine!" said his friends.
"You've bought SO much for you
That we'll get you no presents.
What else can we do?"
Said they, said they, said his friends.

And on Christmas Eve
All under his tree
Were the presents he'd bought.
"Merry Christmas to me!"
Said he, said he, said the pig.

But it wasn't much fun
Giving things to himself.
So he took down his pig bank
That stood on the shelf.
"Let's see, let's see," said the pig.

"I'll go shopping right now,
And I'll spend every dime
To buy my friends presents.
I'm glad there's still time!"
With glee, said he, said that pig.

GREEN CHRISTMAS

1. "It's almost Christmas, and still no snow!"
   Cry the woodland creatures. "We still can go
   Out of our houses to search for roots
   And seeds in the dry grass, and maybe shoots
   Of fern and fennel that think it's spring.
   We may find acorns—'most anything
   That's good to eat may be in sight
   For Christmas dinner, on such a night,
   When the ground is bare of ice and snow,
   And stars are bright, and the winds don't blow.
   Hurrah for Christmas and still no snow!"

2. "It's almost Christmas, and still no snow!"
   Sigh the townsfolk, wishing the wind would blow.
   "Our doors are wreathed with pine and holly,
   And our Christmas trees would look extra jolly
   Blazing with lights—if the snow came down
   Deep and white all over the town!
   Why doesn't the sky go woolly gray?
   Why doesn't it snow for Christmas Day?
   It's not like Christmas without some snow!"
   Sigh the townsfolk, wishing the wind would blow—

3.   BUT—
   "Hurrah for Christmas and still no snow!"
   Cry the woodland creatures, and out they go.

11

MR. HEDGEHOG'S CHRISTMAS FEELING

MR. Hedgehog shook Mrs. Hedgehog.

And Mrs. Hedgehog shook all the little hedgehogs.

"What's wrong?" they asked drowsily.

"Yes," asked Mrs. Hedgehog sleepily, "what's wrong?"

Mr. Hedgehog stretched and grinned.

"Nothing's *wrong*," he said. "It's just that I have the best kind of wonderful feeling. It's the kind of feeling that says:

"There's snow all about and the stars are keen,
And the berries are red and the holly is green,
The bells are ringing such joyous carols—
There's mincemeat soaking in spicy barrels,
Puddings are steaming, rich and tasty,
There's many a cake and many a pasty
Rising, or bubbling syrupy juice,
And many a turkey and many a goose
Is roasting brown in a roasting pan.
I simply DON'T believe I can
Sleep in a burrow underground
With so many Christmas joys around!"

"Very well," smiled Mrs. Hedgehog, merrily shaking moth balls out of her muff.

"Where are we going?" asked the little Hedgehogs. They all reached for their coats.

"To town!" cried Mr. Hedgehog, who had found his Sunday hat. "To London-town!"

He scampered out of the burrow and up the nearest holly tree. There he picked a large sprig of holly for Mrs. Hedgehog's muff, small sprigs for all the little Hedge-hogs' buttonholes, and a very large sprig, bright with berries, to tuck in the band of his own hat.

"Now we are ready to go to London-town," laughed Mr. Hedgehog.

"Ready every one," said Mrs. Hedge-hog.

Then arm in arm, the Hedgehog family hurried through the snowy twilight, head-ing for the lights of Londontown, and the wonderful Christmas sights they would see.

MR. HEDGEHOG'S CHRISTMAS PRESENT

London town was even more wonderful than Mr. Hedgehog had imagined. The stores were a miracle of shining lights and splendid sights!

Even the mice went about with presents for their friends, and "Merry Christmas" on their lips.

"I should like to get a present for Mrs. Hedgehog!" said Mr. Hedgehog to himself.

What should it be?

Not a fur coat. Mrs. Hedgehog had one that suited her perfectly.

Not a diamond tiara. That would be too heavy for her head. Might make it ache!

Surely not a bottle of scent. Hedgehogs like the smell of fern and hawthorne.

14

Suddenly something lovely caught Mr. Hedgehog's eye. A bright red apple lay in the clean snow near the curb, lost and forgotten!

Mr. Hedgehog picked it up and brushed off the snow. He polished it with his mittens.

Solemnly he offered it to his wife. "A Merry Christmas, my dear!" he said.

Mrs. Hedgehog kissed him. "Thank you," she said. "I'll make us a big, sweet, warm apple dumpling of it!"

The little Hedgehogs, one and all, smacked their lips and shouted "Merry Christmas" again and again.

And arm in arm the Hedgehog family hurried home to their cozy burrow, which soon smelled excitingly of apple and spice and crisp pastry browning—

The very merriest kind of Christmas smell!

The Snowshoe Rabbits

FIVE happy rabbits sat close to the fireplace in their snug little house. One was the mother rabbit, one was the daddy rabbit, and three were young rabbits who had never seen Christmas.

"First of all, there will be the tree," said the mother rabbit. "Grandma always has a Christmas tree. It will be dressed with popcorn and berries, and lighted with candles. And on it there will be presents for three good little rabbits!"

The little rabbits' eyes shone just as if the candles were lighted right then.

"And, of course, your Grandpa will play his rabbit piano," grinned the daddy rabbit. "He'll play 'Jingle Bells' and 'Deck the Halls' and 'The First Noël.'"

Now the little rabbits began to hum.

They knew all those songs. They knew all about Christmas at Grandma's. So they sang till their ears waggled.

Then one little rabbit hopped up. He was a fat little rabbit, licking his lips.

"After that comes Christmas dinner," he said. "A big roast carrot basted with sugar, mashed turnips with butter, and cranberries red and shining. And for dessert, a round pudding all lighted up, with holly on top!"

That fat little rabbit flopped back in his chair.

"I can hardly wait for tomorrow," he whispered. "I can hardly wait to go to Grandma's!"

The other little rabbits nodded very hard.

The mother rabbit smiled.

"We'll go early in the morning," said the daddy rabbit, looking at his watch. "And right now it's time good little rabbits were in bed."

"We'll never be able to go to Grandma's now!" said his brother.

And the little girl rabbit pulled her apron over her head to hide her tears.

By and by the three little rabbits crept downstairs. Sorry little rabbits they were, full of gulps and sighs and tears that almost spilled over.

Their mother and daddy didn't seem sad at all. They talked happily all through breakfast, just as if nothing had happened. After breakfast their daddy hurried up to the attic. Back he came, smiling and proud, with some queer-looking things under his arm. They looked like tennis rackets. But who plays tennis in the deep snow?

Nobody.

In the whisk of a whisker all three little rabbits were in their beds and sound asleep.

They dreamed of shining candles
And wonderful presents
And beautiful smells
And a glossy tree
And a sprinkling of snow.

But when they hopped out of bed in the morning and looked out the window, there was no sprinkling of snow.

Sprinkling, indeed!

It had snowed all through the night. Snow covered the hills and the long grass and all the rabbit paths. It was heaped halfway up the house, deeper than boots, deeper than leggings—deeper than the three little rabbits themselves!

"It's too deep!" whispered the fat little rabbit.

"What *are* they?" asked the fat little rabbit at last.

"Snowshoes," laughed the daddy rabbit. "They're for walking right on top of deep snow."

None of the little rabbits waited to hear any more. They scrambled into their warmest clothes. They gathered up all the exciting, secret present packages they had made.

And before very long, out into the crisp white snow went the whole rabbit family. Across the deep snow they tramped in those wonderful snowshoes.

They made big scuffy tracks from their house straight toward their Grandma's house.

And as they went they sang:

Snowshoe rabbits in the snow,
Off to Grandma's house we go—
Holly, pudding, popcorn, toys,
Shining candles, lots of noise;
Off to Grandma's house we go!
Sing for Christmas!
Sing for snow!

19

MOUSE CHRISTMAS

Oh, the wonderful bits
That folks drop as they go,
Cooking and baking
And hurrying so!
Citron and raisins
And powdery spice,
Sugar and currants—
It's nice to be mice

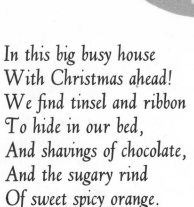

In this big busy house
With Christmas ahead!
We find tinsel and ribbon
To hide in our bed,
And shavings of chocolate,
And the sugary rind
Of sweet spicy orange.

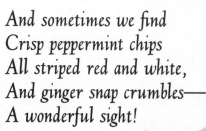

And sometimes we find
Crisp peppermint chips
All striped red and white,
And ginger snap crumbles—
A wonderful sight!

We'll fill up our stockings,
When Christmas Eve comes,
With the savory bits
And the wonderful crumbs;
Citron and raisins
And sugar and spice—
Oh, just before Christmas
It's NICE to be mice!

A VERY SMALL CHRISTMAS

I wonder if the chipmunks know,
    When everything is white with snow
And night starts coming very fast,
    That Christmas time is here at last?

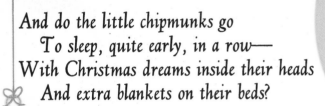

And do the little chipmunks go
    To sleep, quite early, in a row—
With Christmas dreams inside their heads
    And extra blankets on their beds?

And do they hop up just at dawn
    And put their robes and slippers on
And hurry out to peep and see
    If someone brought a Christmas tree?

If someone did, I wonder who?
    Their chimney's small to wriggle through!
Their Christmas tree must be a twig—
    But maybe chipmunks think it's big.
I hope it's trimmed with sunflower seeds,
    And peanuts, too, and icy beads,
And lighted candles (birthday size)
    To make a grand chipmunk surprise!

TERRIBLE TEDDY BEAR

NOW Terrible Teddy Bear did not look like a terrible bear at all. He was the brown kind of teddy bear, just the size to take to bed. And he had a funny little squeak, and shiny black eyes and a bit of a smile. But he WAS a terrible teddy just the same.

Even Santa Claus, who had made this teddy and who had said, "He's the best bear I ever did make!" decided that at last.

"This terrible teddy bear!" he said the first Christmas morning at breakfast. "This terrible teddy bear climbed out of my pack last night. He hid under the seat of my sleigh. When I got back home, there he was—back home too! And not wherever I meant to leave him for some good child!"

"Dear, dear!" said Mrs. Santa Claus.

And she was still saying "Dear, dear!" five Christmases later. Because every Christmas Eve, Terrible Teddy Bear climbed out of the toy pack. Every Christ-

mas Eve he hid in a different place. And every Christmas morning he was back home at the North Pole.

On the fifth Christmas morning Santa Claus made up his mind to do something about Terrible Teddy.

He hurried into his workshop and looked at the letters in the basket marked NO! That basket was chockful of letters from people who didn't deserve presents and did not get presents. Santa Claus always felt very sad when he looked at those letters.

Just the same, he sat down and read them all.

He read straight through lunch and halfway through supper. Then he jumped up, holding a crumpled letter in one red mitten.

"Here is a letter from someone more terrible than Terrible Teddy," he said. "Here is a letter from Terrible Tommy, who says 'I won't' all day long, and eats nothing but candy and bubble gum, and besides—he never will go to bed at night."

"Dear, dear!" said Mrs. Santa Claus. "You can't EVER take him a present!"

"Oh, yes I can," Santa laughed. "I'm going to his house right now—a special trip. And I'm going to give him Terrible Teddy!"

"Dear, dear!" Mrs. Santa Claus said. "Dear, dear, dear, dear, dear, dear, dear, dear!"

But by that time the reindeer were harnessed, the sleigh was out of the barn. And Santa was driving over the roof tops on Christmas night.

He was driving one-handed at that. In his other hand he held Terrible Teddy, tight as tight.

Terrible Teddy certainly didn't look terrible now. He was trying very hard to squeak, "Oh, please don't give me to Terrible Tommy!" But Santa held him too tightly.

Before long the sleigh stopped with a jerk. It stopped on the roof of Tommy's house.

All the lights were out.

Everyone was asleep. Everyone, that is, except Terrible Tommy.

He sat by the hearth, rubbing his eyes and blowing his nose. He sobbed a bit, too.

"Santa Claus didn't come to me," he cried. "He didn't bring me a thing. Not even some ashes and switches. Not even some old, worn, patched britches. Not even a horn that wouldn't blow. Not even anything. Oh, oh, oh! And I wanted a teddy bear, even an old one, a brown and plushy and nice-to-hold one—with shiny eyes in his fuzzy head, the kind that's the size for taking to bed."

Santa Claus, up on the roof, heard Terrible Tommy. He blew some ashes down to make Tommy close his eyes. And when Tommy did—

Whisk! down the chimney came Santa.

Whisk! up he went again, leaving Terrible Teddy behind.

Away went the sleigh with its bells all jingling.

Terrible Tommy opened his eyes—and there, right in front of him, sat Terrible Teddy.

"Santa did come!" cried Tommy. "He made a special trip just for me—and he brought the nicest, softest, best kind of Teddy Bear in the whole world!"

He picked up Terrible Teddy and hugged him tightly. Teddy liked that so much that he hugged back. Tommy liked *that* so much that he felt good from head to toe.

And right then all the Terrible went straight out of Tommy.

It went out of Teddy, too.

Up the stairs they went, both together. Both together they climbed into Tommy's bed. Both together they went sound asleep.

And they looked just like a good little boy sleeping, and a good teddy bear sleeping, too.

By that time, of course, Santa Claus was back at the North Pole.

"Dear, dear, dear," said Mrs. Santa. "I just don't think you should have gone on that special trip. I just don't think you should have taken a present to anyone who is bad!"

Santa Claus chuckled and hung up his hat. He laughed and hung up his coat.

"I'll tell you a secret, Mrs. Santa," he said. "Terrible Tommy isn't bad any more. He's as good as a boy can be. Terrible Teddy isn't bad, either."

Then Santa Claus clapped his knees with pleasure.

"I always did say he was the best bear I ever made," he said. "And it wouldn't be right for Santa Claus to be wrong, would it, now?"

Mrs. Santa Claus didn't say "Dear, dear!"

She said:
"Of course not.
That would
Never
Never
NEVER
Do!"

MR. LION'S PLUM PUDDING

LION read his letter over and over.
"Well, well," he declared at last,
"that's the finest thing I ever heard."
"What is?" asked Mrs. Lion.
"My cousin Barnaby,—you remember

him, my dear? He was, er, captured and
kindly consented to go to America to live
in a zoo. Well, my dear, he says here that
in America they have Christmas. Sounds
like a most wonderful kind of day, full of
presents and snow and candles and candies
and cookies. And probably the best part
of all is the last, which is called plum pudding!"

"What won't they think of next?"
said Mrs. Lion in a sort of faraway voice,
because she was busily cleaning the
kitchen.

"Hmmm," grunted Mr. Lion, reading
his letter just once more. Then he folded
it neatly, put it on the shelf, and rubbed
his chin.

"Mrs. Lion," he said. "Mrs. Lion, we
are going to have Christmas!"

"But I'm just finishing spring house cleaning!" cried Mrs. Lion.

"Never mind that," her husband said, and he began at once to make his plans for Christmas.

"Snow we can't have," he decided. "Presents are out, because I spent my allowance on a beaver hat. Candles and candies and cookies sound lovely, except that I don't know what they are. But plum pudding—now, plum pudding we shall have!"

He opened the cupboards and pulled out bowls. He went to the flour bin and measured flour, spilling it in drifts from one end of the kitchen to the other.

Mrs. Lion grumbled, but Mr. Lion only laughed. "Looks like snow," he said. "Leave it there!"

He stewed plums with sugar until they boiled all over the stove. Then he chopped a bowl of nuts so vigorously that they bounced about the house like popcorn.

"Oh, dear!" sighed Mrs. Lion. "Oh, dear."

"Now for the suet!" cried Mr. Lion.

He took a large chunk from the refrigerator and mixed it with the other good things. He added more sugar and pinches of spice, and handfuls of raisins; and he worked the whole thing into a round, sticky, slippery ball with his paws. That looked like such fun that Mrs. Lion had to try it, too.

She reached for the pudding, and it slid out of Mr. Lion's paws and out of her paws. Mr. Lion's plum pudding rolled round and round the kitchen, picking up sugar and nuts and flour and raisins as it went.

At last it stopped in the corner.

"Looks ready to cook," grinned Mr. Lion. He wrapped the pudding in one of his wife's best napkins, and since he had to go to the linen closet for that, there were floury tracks all through the house.

27

But before long, Mr. Lion's pudding was steaming. Before long, Mr. and Mrs. Lion's house smelled richly of spices and plums and sugar. Several friends, Mr. and Mrs. Camel, Grandfather Bear, and Trump, the youngest elephant, dropped in unexpectedly.

"How nice to see you!" cried Mr. Lion. "How did you happen to come?"

"Just followed our noses," grinned Trump, and his long nose certainly was pointing straight at the pudding.

"The pudding!" Mrs. Lion said. "I do believe it's done!"

She put it on the table, roly-poly and steaming and set about with juicy raisins and plums. Mr. Lion stuck a red flower in the center to serve as holly, and everyone sat down to eat.

"A Merry Christmas to all!" cried Mr. Lion.

All his friends bowed and said Merry Christmas, too. And that plum pudding was so delicious that even Mrs. Lion forgot the fuss and bother it had made in her spring-cleaned house.

She did say later, "Nice as Christmas is, Mrs. Camel, I'm glad it comes only once a year!"

"Not here!" said her husband. "No, indeed. I'm going to find out all about candles and candies and cookies from Barnaby—and THEN we'll have Christmas once every month, at the very least!"

SURPRISE!

The pony was green.
(It's as true as can be!)
The camel was purple.
(A strange sight to see!)
A sugar-white panther
Who looked rather pale
Was resting his paws
On a blue monkey's tail.
The lion was yellow,
As fierce as can be—
"I'll eat you all up
In a one-two-and-three!"
He growled at the others.
But quicker than scat
Somebody said, "Cookies!
And frosted at that!"
Somebody said, "Yummy!"
And reached out a hand
And gobbled the lion,
Who tasted just grand.
He was gone in a wink
(Which is half of a look)
And NOBODY missed him—
Not even the cook!

THE GOAT WHO PLAYED SANTA CLAUS

ONCE upon a time there were five little chicks who thought Santa Claus was sure to come to them. It was the day before Christmas, and they were very much excited.

"He'll bring us a tree of the Christmas kind," they told each other. "And five Christmas presents—one for each!"

Everyone in the barnyard wanted those chicks to have a happy Christmas.

But Grandmother Goose was worried.

And old Turkey Gobbler was very worried.

"Santa Claus never *did* come to us," he said. "I just don't think he comes to barnyards."

"Neither do I," sighed Grandmother Goose. "And what I say is, somebody should *tell* those chicks."

She tied on her shawl.

Old Turkey Gobbler pulled on his cap.

"Come along," he said. "We'll tell them."

But before they had gone two waddles and a strut, fat Uncle Pig hurried up to them.

"Oh no, you don't," he cried. "You're not going to spoil those little chicks' fun!"

The cow agreed.

So did the horse.

"Indeed you won't!" bleated the sheep, running up.

Mother Hen smiled.

"Good!" she cackled. "I just do want my chicks to have a nice Christmas!"

Old Turkey Gobbler snorted.

"All very well," he said. "But what about Christmas morning?"

"What about when they find that Santa *didn't* come?" asked Grandmother Goose.

"Oh," said Mother Hen.

She looked sadly at her yellow chicks, who were skittering around trying to sing "Up on the Housetop" in their peeping voices. She looked even more sadly at her barnyard friends.

"My chicks were so sure Santa Claus would come," she sighed, "that I myself was believing it, too."

The cow and the horse and the sheep sighed deeply.

Grandmother Goose started toward the happy chicks.

But fat Uncle Pig had a sudden and wonderful idea.

He saw the white goat strolling up and down near the clothesline, his snowy beard wagging merrily. He saw the clothes flapping on the line. There were red mittens drying, and a fine suit of the farmer's red underwear. There was a pillow case blowing out, just as if it were a pack full of presents for five little chicks.

"I have a feeling that Santa Claus is really coming to those chicks!" Uncle Pig squealed. "Just you wait and see!"

Then he whispered his wonderful idea to the other animals. Mother Hen was so pleased that she ran in circles until she saw everything twice. The cow and the horse grinned from ear to ear.

"Maybe the goat won't help," sighed Grandmother Goose.

"I'll ask him," smiled the sheep. And she went and talked to the goat.

His eyes twinkled.

"I'd love to do it," he said. "Sounds like fun."

The horse, meanwhile, neatly nipped the clothespins from the red mittens, the red underwear, and the pillowcase, and took them off the line.

Uncle Pig, meanwhile, went looking in the junk heap in back of the barn. He looked very sharply, and what did he find?

Oh, some wonderful things: a small tin bank made like a drum, a little red wagon missing one wheel, a small red mitten with a hole in the thumb, a bright green sock that had no mate, a pair of doll's skates (thrown away by mistake), and bits of spruce branches, too small to use in the farmhouse.

"What else do I need?" he said to himself.

Pussycat Smart came padding up.

"Me," she said. "You need me to help tie those bits into a tree. You need me to fix the little wagon with a new wheel, and to pin up the small mitten's hole in the thumb. And you need me to get some crabapples out of the barrel. We'll hang them on the tree!"

The two worked together.

By the time it was late afternoon, they had made a splendid little tree, and Pussycat Smart had put a new wheel on the wagon.

Then they looked at the presents.

"Rather dirty," mewed Pussycat Smart. "They need a good scrub!"

She ran to fetch Grandmother Goose.

"You're the only one of us who can wash them," she mewed.

Grandmother Goose started to say, "Oh, I'm afraid I can't get them clean!" But just then she saw the fine little Christmas tree.

And just then the white goat came around the barn. He made such a jolly Santa Claus all dressed in the red underwear suit, with the red mittens on his ears for a cap and the pillow case slung over his shoulder, that she laughed.

"I'll polish them spic and span!" she promised.

She washed the presents until they looked like new.

Not to be outdone, old Turkey Gobbler filled the drum and wagon and the one red mitten and the one green sock with chicken corn.

Now everything was ready.

Pretty soon the dusk was dark.

Pretty soon the lights in the farmhouse went out.

Pretty soon the stars were shining, and the five little chicks were fast asleep in the chicken coop.

"It's time to go," whispered the barnyard animals. "Come on, Santa Claus goat!"

"I still have things to do," laughed the goat. "Besides, Santa Claus never comes until everyone is asleep."

"That's right!" all the animals agreed, and they hurried away to their beds. All of them were so glad that Santa Claus was coming to the chicks! But all of them had a wish they were wishing, too.

It was Grandmother Goose who said the wish right out loud.

"I wish Santa Claus would come to me just once," she said, and then she fell asleep.

The Santa Claus goat finished doing the things he still had to do. When he started out, his pack was jammed-crammed full. There seemed to be so much more in it than presents for five little chicks.

Then he tiptoed into the barn and put down his pack.

Out of it he took presents and presents and presents for everyone in the barn.

"A new shawl for Grandmother Goose," he chuckled. "And a basket of apples for the horse. Turnips for the sheep, corn for old Turkey Gobbler, a good smoking pipe for fat Uncle Pig, a catnip mouse for Pussycat Smart, and a bell for Cow. For good Mother Hen, a new blue bonnet——and for me, a rich plum pudding to eat, can and all!"

Very tired he was, the Santa Claus goat, from collecting all those splendid presents. But now the barn looked as exciting as a Christmas tree. He could hardly wait for morning!

"Sleeping's the very best way to get morning to come," the Santa Claus goat told himself wisely.

And he crept quietly into his bed and was soon asleep, still dressed in his funny red Santa Claus suit, and still feeling warm and merry inside from being such a wonderful make-believe Santa Claus.

35

THE GOLDEN SLED

ONCE upon a time, when Christmas was coming, there was a little brown bear who wanted a sled very much. He started to write a letter to Santa Claus, and then he began to wonder what color sled he wanted.

"Let's see," said this little bear. "Let me see. . . . Some bears like red things best. But I'm not that kind of bear. Some bears like blue things. But I'm not that kind of bear, either."

He remembered hearing about a little bear who wanted his whole room painted purple.

"Purple, purple, purple everywhere!" said the little brown bear. "Now I wouldn't like that at all!"

And he began to look all around the dining room, to see what color he liked best. There was a tall white chocolate pot with golden flowers on it. Those flowers were wonderfully shiny! There was a black chair with golden squiggles on the back. It was a gay chair, very nice for rocking oneself. And the little bear thought the golden squiggles made it even nicer.

36

There was a golden clock that ticked merrily—tickety-tock, tockety-tick. And there was a fat round jar with letters on it.

The letters were golden.

They spelled out H-O-N-E-Y.

"Honey!" laughed the little bear. "Golden letters spell honey, and honey is golden—and golden gold is the color I like best!"

So he put that in his letter.

"PLEAZ BRING ME A GOLDEN SLED."

"A golden sled!" said his mother when she saw the letter. "Oh, my! You'll have to be a very good bear to get a *golden* sled!"

"Yes, indeed," said his father. "You'll have to be just as good as gold!"

"Well, I just will!" the little bear said. "I'll just be the very best bear ever."

He brushed his fur suit until it was fluffy and shiny, put on his warm fur cap, and hurried out to mail his letter.

"Oh, my!" said Santa Claus when he read the letter. "A *golden* sled! Well, here's a problem for me! Golden paint is the hardest to get. Golden paint is what I have the least of! And here's a little bear that wants a whole sled painted golden!"

He thought about that while he was making the sled, and he shook his head.

When the sled was all finished (except for paint), Santa Claus looked at his little jar of golden paint.

"It would take every last drop to paint this sled," he said. "I wouldn't have one smidgeon left to put on anybody's engine, or anybody's chair, or anybody's doll-baby's locket!"

And then Santa Claus decided he would have a look at this good little bear who wanted a golden sled.

So he whizzed up his chimney, climbed out on his roof, and sat down. He took out his spy-glass, and pointed it at the little bear's house. He turned it a bit this way, and a bit that way, to see better.

Now Santa Claus could see the little bear. And oh, my! he could hardly believe his eyes!

37

First he saw the little bear making his own bed, neat and tidy, tight as a drum.

Then he saw the little bear eating his breakfast, good as gold, with a yum-yum-yum.

He saw the little bear drying the dishes
And putting them away
And sweeping the porch
And putting all the rubber boots in a row, easy to find.

Santa Claus saw the little bear going to the store with a long list, and not forgetting anything.

He saw that little bear helping old bears across the street
And minding baby bears for their mothers
And saying "yes, ma'am" and "no, sir" with the kindest and most friendly of smiles.

And all this time Santa Claus could see the little bear's good little heart shining right through his furry coat! It was dancing a happy dance, thumpity-thump—and it was a shining heart, golden as golden, because the little bear was SO good.

"Well, I declare," cried Santa Claus. "This little bear, this good little bear who wants a golden sled, has a heart of gold!"

That made Santa Claus think twice.

He whizzed down his chimney and took his little jar of golden paint in one hand. Then he searched in his paint box, and way down at the bottom he found a little jar of silver paint, too.

"That does it!" he grinned. "I can put silver on all the engines, instead of gold. I can put silver on all the chairs. And this year, everybody's doll baby will have a silver locket instead of a golden one!"

Humming to himself, Santa Claus dipped a brush into the golden paint and began to paint the little bear's sled. When the little jar of paint was empty, with not a smidgeon of paint left, the sled was all painted shiny, bright, glittering, glistening, sparkling gold!

And when the good little bear woke up on Christmas morning and put on his slippers and scampered downstairs—
There was his sled under the tree—
Golden as golden!

"Oh, lovely!" he whispered. "And I never did think I'd get a whole golden sled. I never did think I could be good enough!"

His mother kissed him and said, "Why, you're the best little bear in the whole world!"

His father patted his head and said, "Yes, sir, you're just as good as gold!"

The little brown bear said "Merry Christmas" to his father and mother.

He put on his mittens and cap and boots.

He took his shining golden sled out into the snowy Christmas day.

And he went coasting down the white hill.

Past the dark green trees
Thinking—
"A great big, bright and golden Merry Christmas to everybody in every place in this whole big shining world!"

THE SECRET RIDE

IT was very late on Christmas night. The barn was dark, and most of the animals were asleep. But not the new Christmas pony. He peeped out at the house. The house was dark, too, and everyone in it was asleep.

The pony turned his glossy head and looked proudly at the new red Christmas sleigh.

His eyes shone, just looking at it.

How fast he had pulled that sleigh all day! How the bells had jingled, and how the children had laughed and shouted and sung! What fun it had been trotting swiftly through the snow with that splendid sleigh!

The pony had wished he could go on and on around the farm, over the hill, across the frozen brook, forever.

"I wish I could go out right now," he thought. "I'd like to see how it feels in the dark with the stars shining and the icy trees glistening, and the wind still and the snow crisp and dry."

He shook his small head impatiently. He winked one eye gaily. And he looked merrily at the lamb and the ducks, the pigs and the calf, the drowsy hens and the brave little rooster.

"Why not?" he asked himself. "Why not take *them* for a ride in the Christmas sleigh?"

He nudged the rooster and whispered,
"Want to go for a sleigh ride?"

In one second the rooster was wide
awake.

"Oh, yes!" he cried.

He crowed a loud crow that awakened
all the others. In two seconds they had
climbed and scrambled and flapped and
clambered into the shiny red sleigh.

"Here we go!" the pigs squealed.

"Merry Christmas!" bleated the lamb.
The hens chuckled and the rooster
crowed.

But the Christmas pony said "Oh!" in
a surprised way.

"How am I to hitch myself to the
sleigh?" he asked. "I don't know how!"

"Oh!" cried the other animals. "Oh,
sad Christmas! What a disappointment!"

And then Pussycat Smart came padding
up.

"I know how," she purred. "I'll do the
hitching if I can do the driving."

Nobody argued the least bit about that.
And before long, Pussycat Smart had the
Christmas sleigh hitched to the Christmas
pony. She had the barn doors open, and
she sat in the sleigh, holding the reins.

Five little mice came whisking out of
the hay.

"We want to go, too!" they squeaked.

For a moment Pussycat Smart licked her whiskers. "Oh, yes, my dears," she thought greedily. "You're welcome to go—inside me!"

But after all, it *was* Christmas.

After all, she was quite stuffed with tasty scraps from the table.

"Come along, then," she mewed, slapping the reins until the bells tinkled like hundreds of stars tumbling out of the sky. "Come along, then, you five."

The mice found seats in the folds of the warm fur rug.

The pony pranced lightly across the barn floor.

Then out of the barn went that happy, jingling sleighful of animals. Over the snow they raced, squeaking and bleating, mooing and crowing, cackling and squeaking for joy.

All around the farm they went, in a big zig-zagging line, under the stars, under the glistening trees. They sped across the frozen brook six times for the sport of skidding on the ice. And they went singing up and down the hill.

At last, with their noses and beaks and bills red with cold, they came back to the snug barn.

Pussycat Smart unharnessed the Christmas pony and locked the barn door. The lamb rubbed the snowflakes off the Christmas sleigh. The calf licked the runners dry and shining. The hens folded the warm fur rug, taking orders from the rooster. And the five little mice scurried to bed.

Soon all the animals were in bed, warm and sleepy and happy.

"Everything's tidy," whispered the Christmas pony. "Everything's back in place. Nobody ever will know that I took all the animals for a secret ride on Christmas night."

But that sleepy little pony quite forgot all the extra tracks he had made in the crisp white snow.

Surely the children would see them!

Surely they would wonder about those wild zig-zagging tracks!

Surely they would guess all about that secret ride on Christmas night—and love the new Christmas pony even more for giving a wonderful sleigh ride to all his new friends in the friendly barn!

THE COLD LITTLE SQUIRREL

1 Once there was a little squirrel who was cold—morning, noon, and night—all winter long.

2 But at night he was coldest. And on Christmas Eve, br–r–r! he could not sleep.

3 Out of his house he crept. He sat on a snowy branch, shivering under the stars.

4 "Colder than ever," he said. "But it seems sort of magic, too." Down the tree he ran.

44

5 He scampered across the snow. "Maybe I'll find a warm magic coat," he said. "Maybe, warm boots."

6 Not a thing did he find on that still, magic night. But suddenly he saw something far away.

7 It was a small, cozy house, its windows bright with candles.

The little squirrel ran to it and climbed up on the chimney.

8 Close to the hearth sat a fluffy little raccoon. She was saying to her mother, "I wish Santa would bring me a real live doll!"

9 And just at that moment the cold little squirrel slipped on the ice. Right down the chimney he tumbled!

10 The little raccoon picked him up and hugged him.

"Here's my real live doll!" she cried. "I'll make him a warm little coat and warm boots!"

11 And the cold little squirrel curled up in her arms, cozy and warm on that cold, still, magic night.

THE BARE POLAR BEAR

NOW once upon a time there was a big, white, fluffy polar bear who wanted very much to be one of Santa Claus's helpers. Time after time, he knocked on the workshop door and asked if he couldn't please do something to help.

But time after time, the answer he got was no, and thank you most kindly just the same.

The helpers all agreed he was MUCH too big to be a helper. Mrs. Santa Claus said it wouldn't do at all. And Santa himself was too busy to even look up from his work.

At last, only three days before Christmas, the big, white, fluffy polar bear gave up trying. "I'll never get to be a helper," he told himself. "It's no use trying!"

And strangely enough, at that very same moment, Santa Claus was saying "It's no use trying," too!

"There are hundreds of stores where I'm supposed to say hello to the children," he told Mrs. Santa, "and hundreds and hundreds of corners where I'm supposed to ring bells. And the toys aren't quite finished. And besides, there are so many good children this year that I have more chimneys to slide down than ever before!"

Santa Claus said he simply could NOT be everywhere at once. He said it was no use trying.

Mrs. Santa Claus thought very hard.

"Your helpers will be glad to go to the stores and ring the bells for you," she said. "I'll fit them all out in your old Santa Claus suits!"

Up to the attic she ran. In a twinkling, she had the helpers all dressed up in fine, red suits, with pillows for round, jolly tummies.

At first Santa Claus thought they looked splendid.

Then he thought there was something missing.

"Beards!" he cried at last. "They have no beards!"

"Oh, dear!" sighed Mrs. Santa. "They can't go without beards, and there's no time to grow beards. And I have no old Santa Claus beards in the attic, because *you've* always had such a beautiful beard growing right out of your chin!"

"Oh, oh, oh, what are we to do?" cried all the helpers, so sadly that the sound went up the chimney and echoed from iceberg to iceberg all over the North Pole.

Everybody heard it.

And especially a big white fluffy polar bear heard it.

He ran straight to the workshop and knocked on the door. Mrs. Santa Claus opened the door and in he went, white and fluffy, sparkling with snow.

"Anything I can do to help?" he asked.

Everyone looked at his fluffy white fur.

"Beards!" whispered Mrs. Santa Claus.

"Wonderful beards!" chuckled Santa himself.

The helpers told the bear their troubles.

"And please, Mr. Bear," they asked. "May we snip off some of your fluffy white fur for beards?"

The bear bowed. "To be sure!" he said.

Mrs. Santa Claus took her scissors. She snipped here and there while the polar bear stood very still.

"More!" cried the helpers, busily making beards.

More!

More!

More!

Snip! Snip! Snip! went the scissors.

Stitch! Stitch! Stitch! went the helpers.

Before long there were enough fluffy white beards for every single helper.

BUT—

"G–g–g–gracious!" shivered the polar bear. "Don't you think it's turning c–c–c–cold?"

Everyone looked at that nice fluffy polar bear. He wasn't one bit fluffy now. He hadn't a snippet of warm white fur left. All his fur had gone for beards. And he

was shivering and shaking just like the very bare bear he was!

He looked so funny that even Santa wanted to laugh.

"But it's no laughing matter!" he told himself. "This bear will get sniffles without his fur!"

"Couldn't you just sit here by the fire till your fur grows again, Mr. Bear?" asked one helper.

The polar bear looked at his bare paw.

"Well," he sighed. "I did want to go about singing carols. I'm known for my voice, you know. And I did so want to get a Christmas tree for my three little bears. And I'm sure Mrs. Polar Bear would hate me to miss Christmas dinner."

Big tears came to his eyes.

The helpers pulled off their beards and said, "We'll glue your fur back on!"

49

But at that very moment Mrs. Santa Claus came hurrying up with a measuring tape.

She measured the polar bear.

She cut up a very large piece of red flannel.

She sewed on her whirring sewing machine.

And she put a zipper in what she was making.

When what she was making was made, she helped the polar bear to try it on. It was a most wonderful warm red snow suit, just the right size for the bear. He zipped the zipper, and drew up the hood—and there was that polar bear all cozy and warm again.

He jumped in the air and clicked his heels together. He kissed Mrs. Santa and shook hands with the helpers. He waved to Santa Claus and away he went, eager to show Mrs. Polar Bear his fine new suit.

The helpers put on their beards and hurried off to say hello to the children in the stores and to ring bells on corners.

Mrs. Santa baked a big round coffee cake with raisins and icing, and put on a pot of coffee.

And after supper, Santa Claus finished Susie Hopkins' new doll.

"Time for bed!" said Mrs. Santa.

Santa Claus yawned, but he shook his head.

"I'm making three little stuffed polar bears that squeak," he said, picking up bits of polar bear fur. "They're for Mr. Bear's three little boys."

"I do declare you *are* a saint!" smiled Mrs. Santa Claus proudly.

And she sat down beside her husband to make three little red snow suits with zippers for the three little stuffed polar bears that Santa Claus was making for a Christmas surprise.

THE GOOSE THAT STUFFED HERSELF

OW Tobias Tiger was extremely fond of his family. Nothing pleased him so much as to fetch home a surprise

be it a bag of molasses taffy—
or a bit of gay ribbon—
or a fine, juicy soup bone.

A surprise of any kind, tucked in his vest pocket, hidden under his jacket, or slipped up his sleeve, made him grin from one striped ear straight across to the other.

So with Tobias Tiger.

And when he came home, early one gray evening halfway between Thanksgiving and Christmas, with a rather scrawny gray goose—well! you'd have thought that Tobias had fetched home the moon.

He flopped the gray goose, quite limp with struggling, on the kitchen table and rocked proudly back on his heels.

"Poor thing!" cried Mrs. Tiger (whose name was Tabitha), eying the goose. "Poor thing! It does look cold!"

She wrapped it warmly in her own red shawl and rocked it a bit in her Boston rocker.

The little boy tigers patted its sides.

"A very thin goose, isn't it, Papa?" they asked.

Tobias Tiger tried not to look cross.

"Cold it may be, thin it may be," he said, unwrapping his muffler. "But we'll fatten it up and roast it to a turn—and a splendid dinner it will make us on Christmas day."

Mrs. Tiger stopped rocking the goose.

"What a dandy surprise, Mr. Tiger!" she cried. And she plumped the goose onto

51

her largest platter to see how it would look.

"With a garnish of parsley—" said Tobias Tiger.

"And plenty of stuffing," said his striped sons, "it will make as pretty a goose as ever was eaten!"

At that the goose flipped herself over and began to lick the platter hungrily.

"Can't begin fattening her too soon," Mrs. Tiger observed. She mixed corn meal with milk and stirred it over the fire.

The goose began to eat.

She ate until she was happy.

She ate until she was warm.

She ate until she could not keep one eye open, let alone two.

Then she flapped happily into Mrs. Tiger's lap, tucked her head under the red shawl, and snored loudly.

Mrs. Tiger rocked her gently. The little boy tigers talked in whispers. And Tobias Tiger (ready for bed in his striped pajamas) said good night in a sort of snort and went upstairs.

Before many days had passed, that goose had made herself one of the family.

She followed Roger Tiger about as if she were a dog. She slept on the foot of Will Tiger's bed. She watched the pots and kettles for Mrs. Tiger. And the minute dinner was ready, she honked a happy honk that was better than a gong or bell.

"I do think she should be allowed to eat with us," whispered Mrs. Tiger. "She could sit in Will's old high chair."

Tobias Tiger put his foot down.

"Indeed she'll not!" he shouted. "She'll eat corn meal behind the stove like a fattening Christmas goose!"

Eat corn meal she did. And by the time Christmas was only a week away, that goose was the plumpest, waddlingest,

most mouth-watering goose in the whole white winter world. Tobias Tiger, who was hiding surprises every night now, thought she was the best surprise he had ever brought home.

Roger and Will and Mrs. Tiger thought so, too. But not in quite the same way.

"I've made her a warm red cape and bonnet for Christmas," whispered Mrs. Tiger.

Will said he had made her a wooden eating bowl. And Roger had drawn her a picture of herself, very like her, on a long piece of paper to make room for her neck.

But Tobias Tiger's only concern was how to stuff the Christmas Goose.

"Chestnuts," he decided one night in bed.

The next night he thought, no, bread and celery.

"But I do like a bit of onion," he muttered the following night. Chestnuts and bread and celery and onion swam about in his head.

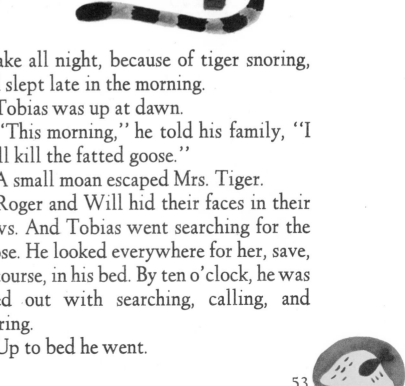

"I can't sleep!" he cried, throwing his pillow on the floor.

Mrs. Tiger brought him another.

"No better!" he shouted.

Roger brought his fluffy pillow and Will brought his puffy pillow.

"No good," sighed Tobias, wide awake. He would still be awake no doubt, except that the goose slipped through the dark and snuggled under his head. She was awake all night, because of tiger snoring, and slept late in the morning.

Tobias was up at dawn.

"This morning," he told his family, "I shall kill the fatted goose."

A small moan escaped Mrs. Tiger.

Roger and Will hid their faces in their paws. And Tobias went searching for the goose. He looked everywhere for her, save, of course, in his bed. By ten o'clock, he was tired out with searching, calling, and roaring.

Up to bed he went.

53

Down he lay. "Lovely, warm, soft pillow," he murmured. "Wouldn't be without it."

Just then the goose stirred and flapped her wings sleepily.

Tobias Tiger leaped out of bed.

"It's you!" he shouted. "It was you all the time!"

The goose smiled sweetly, nodded her head, and went back to her dreams.

"Please don't call our goose 'you,' Papa," whispered Will. "We've named her Tabitha Two, after Mama."

Mrs. Tiger smiled shyly.

And Tobias put on his boots and muffler. Out he went, looking for a surprise. Back he came, with a whopping big turkey all stuffed with chestnuts and bread and celery and onions, and roasted to a turn.

"There," he said proudly. "There's your Christmas dinner. I hope you think it's a good surprise."

"We do," cried Roger and Will and Mrs. Tabitha Tiger all together, hugging him from every side.

Tabitha Two made a noise that sounded like "A superlatively lovely good surprise!"

And on Christmas day she sat at the table in Will's old high chair. She wore her red cape and bonnet. She ate from her new wooden bowl; and she stuffed herself with turkey until she was twice as plump and smiling as the picture Roger had done of her for a special Christmas surprise.

TABITHA TWO

A VERY BIG CHRISTMAS

TRUMPET

was a big, friendly elephant who lived all alone in a small zoo. He loved all the children who came to see him, and he listened to everything they said to each other.

So Trumpet knew that boys play marbles in the springtime, and girls jump rope. He knew about picnics and swimming in the summer. He knew all about raking leaves into a big pile, and jumping in them in the fall. And he had heard what fun it is to watch the leaves burn, how they make a lovely light and the fine, sharp autumn smell of smoke.

All this Trumpet knew.

And he knew something else.

He knew about Christmas in the winter—and about Santa Claus and his reindeer and his tiny sleigh all filled with toys.

"Oh ho," thought Trumpet, all alone in his big cage. "I know what I want for Christmas. I want somebody to keep me company."

He thought about that very hard.

In fact, he thought about it too hard.

Toward Christmas, he began to forget to eat.

Sometimes he even forgot to listen to all the things the children said to each other. And he stood with his back to them, dreaming and rocking to and fro.

The children were troubled by Trumpet's strange new ways. They asked the zoo keeper what was the matter.

"Well," said the zoo keeper, "I think Trumpet is lonesome. I think he needs someone to keep him company."

"If that's all," the children cried, "we can help Trumpet!"

They saved all their pennies for weeks.

They put on a Christmas show "for the benefit of Trumpet" and got hundreds of pennies for tickets.

They sold Christmas cards—

Shoveled snow off peoples' walks and driveways—

And ran errands at a penny an errand.

By and by, those children had the biggest pile of pennies you ever saw!

They took them to the zoo in wagons and doll carriages and wheelbarrows. Then they whispered mysteriously with the zoo keeper.

"No," they said.

And "Maybe"—

And at last, "Yes, yes, yes! That's the VERY thing!"

feeling very tired by now, "maybe Santa Claus doesn't come to animals in the zoo. Maybe I won't get any present at all!"

That was a sad thought for Christmas Eve.

Trumpet squeezed his eyes shut to keep back the tears.

The zoo was quiet now. All the other animals were sleeping.

For a moment Trumpet thought he could hear the snow falling outside. For a moment he thought he heard the stars making a noise like Fourth of July sparklers.

And then he didn't even *think* he heard anything.

Trumpet was sound asleep.

"At last!" whispered the zoo keeper. "Now for his Christmas surprise!"

On Christmas Eve, the zoo keeper tried to get Trumpet to sleep as soon as it was dark. Trumpet lay down in his straw bed, good as gold. But he did not feel one bit like sleeping.

He was much too excited about Christmas. He stared into the dark, wondering what Santa Claus would bring him.

"Maybe a boy to live with me," he thought. "Or maybe a girl."

But no, boys and girls have mothers who want to tuck them into their own beds at night.

"Maybe he'll bring me a pony," thought Trumpet.

But no, not even Santa Claus could find a pony big enough for an elephant to ride!

"Maybe," thought Trumpet, who was

Tramp-tramp-tramp! went some very big feet.

"Shush, shush, shush!" said the zoo keeper.

He led a very large, dark shadow through the dark, sleeping zoo. He opened the door of Trumpet's cage without making one single jingle of keys. And the big shadow tiptoed in, lay down right behind Trumpet, sighed a happy sigh, and went to sleep, too.

When it was morning, Trumpet woke up very early.

He rubbed his eyes and looked all around in the front of his cage.

"Oh," he cried. "Santa Claus *doesn't* come to animals in the zoo! He didn't come to me: He didn't bring me anything at all!"

And just as he said that, Trumpet felt something big and warm behind him. The big and warm something woke up and moved and smiled.

"Hello, Trumpet," it said.

Trumpet turned around.

There, right in his very own cage was a beautiful big gray elephant, with a big red bow on her neck and a sprig of holly in the bow, and a card with squiggles written on it.

"I wonder what the squiggles say?" whispered Trumpet shyly.

"I know," said the new elephant, "because the children read them out loud."

She told Trumpet that the card said:

THIS is CLARindA, YOUR NEW WiFE, WiTH A MERRY CHRISTMAS to TRUMPET because WE LoVE HiM .... FROM ALL THE CHILDREN

Trumpet just smiled and smiled and smiled when he heard that.

And then his heart turned a big somersault, because Clarinda said, "I love you, too, Trumpet."

That was a wonderfully happy thought for Christmas!

"Why," said Trumpet, "why, it's even BETTER than having Santa Claus come!"

Clarinda nodded her head and smiled.

"Much better," she agreed. "If Santa Claus had brought me, he'd have had no room in his pack for one single toy!"

"That's right!" cried Trumpet, laughing at the very thought of his beautiful big new wife riding in Santa's tiny sleigh.

He made Clarinda laugh, too. They laughed until everyone in the whole zoo was awake and calling "Merry Christmas" back and forth.

And one Christmas—
Not *that* Christmas—
Not the next Christmas—
But the *next* Christmas after, Trumpet and his wife had a little baby elephant.

They asked the zoo keeper to put a ribbon on its neck, and a card that said,

MERRY CHRISTMAS
To ALL THE CHILDREN
BECAUSE **WE** LOVE THEM
....TRUMPET AND
      CLARINDA

The keeper did.

And when the children saw that cute, funny, gay little elephant baby, they were almost happier than Trumpet and Clarinda themselves.

Almost, but not quite, because those two big elephants were filled with happiness from their big ears to their big toes.

And NOBODY could ever be happier than two elephants-full!

59

THE CHRISTMAS PUPPY

ONCE there was a puppy who lived in an alley between two brick walls. He ate whatever he found to eat, and he slept in a small empty box.

"It's quite a good bed," said the little puppy.

But one morning he woke up shivering. It was cold in the empty box. The north wind blew through the cracks and cried, "Get up, little puppy! It's winter now and you'll have to find a warmer home."

"That's just what I'll do," barked the little puppy, as he tumbled out of the empty box. "This is the day before Christmas. I'll find a nice warm home for my Christmas present."

He ran out of the alley looking for a warm new home.

When he saw some boys throwing snowballs, he ran right up to them. "Who wants a puppy for Christmas?" he barked.

But the boys only laughed and threw more snowballs. One snowball knocked the little puppy over and over in the snow. He scrambled to his feet.

And when the puppy tried to follow him, he said, "No, little puppy, you can't go home with me. I have no home either."

"Silly puppy," the wind whispered as it came back with a whooosh!

Now the little puppy ran up to the mailman, who was tramping along with his mail bag full of letters and packages.

"I thought boys liked puppies," he thought sadly.

Just then the wind came whistling around the corner. It blew up under the puppy's fur and shook his little ears until they looked like unraveling socks.

"Boys do like puppies," laughed the wind, "but they throw snowballs, too."

The wind twirled the puppy around so he could see a man sitting on a bench. When the puppy ran to him, the man got up and shuffled off through the snow.

"Oh, no, puppy," cried the mailman. "I can't take care of you. I have too many things to take care of already."

The wind blew the puppy out into the slippery street.

"Some people are too busy with packages to bother with little puppies," it whistled, and it tossed the puppy up against a policeman's big foot.

"Here, you," the policeman said. "Get back on the sidewalk before you get hurt."

He put the puppy on a big pile of snow on the sidewalk. There the little puppy felt colder than ever.

It was getting dark, and the lights were coming on in all the stores. People hurried by with their arms full of packages. They laughed in the merriest way, but no one noticed the little puppy.

"Everybody seems too busy to even look at me," he sighed.

And then a little girl ran up to him.

"Oh, Mother," she cried, "look at this darling puppy. Can't I take him home?"

The little puppy's heart leaped for joy.

And then it fell down into his cold little toes, because her mother said:

"A puppy would tear up your dollhouse and scratch the rugs and break all the ornaments on the Christmas tree. Come along!"

The little girl ran back to her mother, and they hurried away in the falling snow.

The wind blew sleet in the puppy's ear.

"Some people have too many things to bother with puppies," sighed the wind as it tumbled him over and over again.

The puppy ran on among hundreds of people and double-hundreds of feet, tramping through the snow. Children scampered from store to store looking at toys in the windows.

"I hope I get that engine," cried a little boy. And a little girl sighed, "I think I will get that beautiful doll!"

"Bow-wow!" barked the little puppy. "Doesn't anybody at all want me for Christmas?"

But only the wind answered him.

"Shush! Some people are too busy wishing to bother with puppies!"

And it pushed him down a side street. The little puppy tried to run into the firehouse, but the wind pushed him back.

"Not there," said the wind. "They have a dog and five little puppies now!"

It blew him past the police station and across the railroad tracks . . . just ahead of a big engine that screamed "Loooooook out! Here I come!"

And then the wind blew the little puppy right out into the country.

It was dark now. The houses were far apart and the snow was deep.

"Oh, dear," he thought, "if I don't find somebody who wants a puppy pretty soon, Christmas will be gone."

"Hurry then," cried the wind, and it blew his woolly ears right out in front of his face.

He ran over a bridge and down a hill. He ran past houses with Christmas trees shining in the windows, with wreaths on the doors and smoking chimneys. Then he saw a dark little house with no Christ-mas tree in its window, no wreath hung on its door.

"Here, puppy," growled the wind. "If you're bound to be a Christmas present, you should have some Christmas wrappings, too."

It blew a bright piece of red ribbon toward him, and laughed and laughed as it whirled away.

The puppy grabbed the Christmas ribbon and began jumping toward the door of the dark house. The trailing ribbon made two straight tracks from the sidewalk right up to the door.

The puppy barked and barked on the doorstep. But no one opened the door.

"I guess nobody is home," he sighed.

He was too tired to go any farther. So he turned round and round to make a little hollow place for lying down, and then—

A big blanket of snow slid off the roof on top of the little puppy! It covered every bit of him and only the ends of the Christmas ribbon showed where he was.

"I'll freeze to an icicle," thought the little puppy. "I'll never live until I'm somebody's Christmas present! I'll never have a home at all!"

Then he heard voices near the road.

"Oh, Mother," cried a little boy's voice. "Santa Claus came while we were out. See the marks of his sleigh!"

His mother looked down at the ribbon tracks.

"I don't think those are sleigh tracks," she said in a tired way. "I just don't think Santa Claus would come away out here."

But the little boy was sure something magic had happened. He went running up the path.

And then he saw the Christmas ribbon sticking up in the snow. He scooped the puppy out of that snowdrift, red ribbon, cold paws, and all, and held him up for his mother to see.

Then the little boy snuggled that cold little puppy against his woolly jacket.

The tired mother smiled a real smile and ran up the path. Her eyes looked as bright as Christmas tree lights. She put her arms around the little boy and the little puppy.

"You did get your present after all," she whispered to her little boy. "Your little Christmas puppy!"

The puppy waggled his icy tail and wiggled his snowy ears and barked.

And the wind laughed merrily.

"Some people are glad to have cold little puppies for Christmas," it said, and away it blew.

THE ONE RED BIRD

ﾟNE red bird would not go south.

"Not I," said he. "The south is bright with flowers and fruit and the songs of birds. But the north is cold and still. Only the black, bare trees stand in the snow against gray sky.

"I will stay here.

"I will flash my bright feathers against the gray sky. I will sing in the quiet winter in the bare black trees.

"I will stay.

"I will stay."

But the wind blew cold—oh, cold.

The snow fell deep and white. It covered the grasses with their dry pods of seeds. The branches were ice-clad, cold and slippery to small bird feet.

Cold—oh, cold.

"What shall I do?" cried the one red bird.

The stars sang coldly.

Under the eaves clung the one red bird. And a little warm draft blew his ruffled feathers. Down he darted to a snowy window sill. The window was open—just enough for a small red bird to squeeze himself through.

Down he flapped to a warm house floor.

And across the room, shining with lights, stood a Christmas tree.

"For me! For me!" sang the one red bird.

He sat on the branches of spicy fir in the shining light.

Popcorn to eat!

And salted nuts!

A gingerbread man up near the top!

"Oh, I'll sing and I'll sing and I'll never stop," sang the one red bird on Christmas Eve in the glittering, glistening, shining light of the Christmas tree.

"For me! For me!" sang the one red bird.

"I will stay."

65

THE CHRISTMAS TREE LAMB

ONCE upon a time there was a small, white, Christmas tree lamb.

He belonged to a grandmother when she was a little girl. He belonged to a mother, too, when she was small.

And when he belonged to the grandmother, he was a brand-new lamb. His fleece was snowy white against the dark branches of the tree. His black bead eyes shone with lights and excitement. And his shining hooves looked as if he might frolic from branch to branch the very next minute.

Besides all that, the tiny golden bell on his collar jingled merrily whenever anyone brushed against the tree.

That was splendid, that first Christmas!

The lamb was new. And the grandmother was little. And everyone said, "The lamb is the prettiest thing on the whole tree!"

There were lots of splendid Christmases.

But after a while, the lamb began to look dusty. After a while the grandmother was grown up. Then the Christmas lamb belonged to the mother.

She loved that lamb when she was little.

She played with him every year before she put him on the tree.

And one year, pop! one bead eye came loose and rolled into a corner.

The next year, crack! the Christmas lamb lost a leg.

Three years later, his tiny golden bell fell off, and was lost with the lost things of Christmas.

By the time the mother was grown up and had a little girl of her own, that lamb was in a sorry state!

He was gray with dust, and he had but one eye, two legs, no collar, and of course, no bell. But he was still a Christmas lamb, eagerly waiting to go on the tree.

The grandmother picked him up and said, "We can't put him on the tree any more!"

The mother took him and said, "No, he's nothing to look at now. But how pretty he was, long ago!"

Now the little girl reached out her hands for the lamb.

"How did he look?" she asked.

The grandmother told about his snowy white fleece.

The mother told about the golden bell that had jingled so merrily.

And the little girl could see for herself that a lamb should have *two* black eyes and *four* shining hooves.

So she took the lamb into her own room. She brushed and cleaned him until he was as white as the snow falling outside. She made him two new legs, and glued them on, and painted them shining black. She sewed a small black bead in place for an eye.

And she tied a bit of red ribbon around the snowy lamb's neck, with a new little golden bell in front.

When Christmas Eve came, the little girl crept downstairs with the lamb held behind her back.

She waited until the grandmother wasn't looking.

She waited until the mother wasn't looking.

Then she stood on a chair, and put the lamb on the Christmas tree, up near the top, right under the shining star.

When the grandmother saw the lamb, her eyes glistened. "He looks just as he did when I was a little girl," she said in a whisper.

The mother looked then, and her eyes sparkled.

"He looks much finer than he did when I was little!" she said.

The little girl didn't say a word.

She was too busy loving the lamb and thinking he was the prettiest thing on the tree. She touched the tree, and the lamb swayed to and fro. His two eyes shone with lights and excitement. His four hooves looked ready to caper from branch to branch.

And his new golden bell jingled more merrily than the old one ever had. Perhaps that was because the small, white Christmas tree lamb was happier than he had ever been in all his white cotton years on all the Christmas trees!

C D E F G H I J